Butterflies
Under Our Hats

Sandy Eisenberg Sasso

Illustrations by Joani Keller Rothenberg

PARACLETE PRESS

BREWSTER, MASSACHUSETTS

There is hope for your future, says the Lord.
(Jeremiah 31:17)

To
Dana and David
and
Debbie and Brad
Be each other's hope.
Grow in each other's love.
SES

To
My children's grandparents
Jack and Julie Keller
and
Gerald and Marlene Rothenberg
who continually fill their dreams with hope and joy.
JKR

Butterflies Under Our Hats
2006   First Printing

Text copyright 2006 by Sandy Eisenberg Sasso
Illustrations copyright 2006 by Joani Keller Rothenberg

ISBN 1-55725-474-5

Library of Congress Cataloging-in-Publication Data
Sasso, Sandy Eisenberg.
  Butterflies under our hats / by Sandy Eisenberg Sasso; illustrations by
  Joani Keller Rothenberg.
       p. cm.
  Summary: Chelm is a town that has lost its luck until the day a beautiful red-haired woman with a purple hat shows the residents something better.
ISBN 1-55725-474-5
[1. Luck—Fiction. 2. Hope—Fiction. 3. Jews—Poland—Fiction.] I. Rothenberg, Joani, 1964-, ill. II. Title.
  PZ7.S24914Bu 2006
  [E]—dc22   2005058667

10 9 8 7 6 5 4 3 2 1

Published by Paraclete Press
Brewster, Massachusetts
www.paracletepress.com
Printed in Singapore

Once there was a town called Chelm
where there was no luck.
If something could go wrong, it did.

The roofs of the houses always leaked.
The sidewalks were cracked.

The gardens grew only weeds.
Nothing was ever right.

Some people said,
"Luck comes and goes."
But in Chelm's case
it never came; it only went.

Others said,
"There is no such thing as luck."
The people of Chelm were certain
that luck was real,
and somewhere they had lost it.

They looked everywhere—

in beds

and in basements,

in pant pockets
and in pickle barrels,

in water wells
and wicker baskets.

But as luck would have it,
they never found any.

"We never have any luck," they sighed.
And so they gave up. They stopped building houses,

delayed repairing sidewalks, and quit planting gardens.

Then one day, a strange and beautiful woman came to town. No one had ever seen her before. She wore a large purple felt hat over her red hair and a long green dress that matched her eyes. She told the people of Chelm that there was something better than luck.

Better than luck? The people weren't sure they believed her, but they listened anyway. Having lost their luck, what else did they have to lose?

"Tomorrow at daybreak," the strange woman with the purple hat and green eyes informed the town, "butterflies of hope are going to fly into the town square. If you can manage to cover the butterflies with your hats, you will have hope, and hope is better than luck."

Some of the townspeople thought the woman was crazy. Nothing was better than luck. But others weren't so sure.

The next morning, just as the sun began to rise, the people of Chelm who couldn't find any luck, went into the town square, to look for hope.

Just as the red-haired, green-eyed woman had said, clouds of colorful butterflies appeared. They landed on the ground.

For a few moments they just sat there;
their wings fluttered softly. The people were very quiet.

They gently placed their hats over the butterflies. There were silk top hats and woolen caps, black berets and bonnets with bows. There were felt fedoras and high hats with pink polka dots.

There were fancy fur hats and silly straw hats with feathers—
all covering the town square.
"We have it!" they all exclaimed. "Now we have hope!"
But just as they said those words, it began to rain.

The drizzle became a downpour and suddenly the people needed their hats. One by one they took their silk top hats and woolen caps, their black berets and bonnets with bows, their felt fedoras and high hats with pink polka dots, their fancy fur hats and their silly straw ones with feathers.

One by one the butterflies disappeared.

They watched as the last person lifted his hat
and the very last butterfly flapped its wings and
rose into the sky.
"Now not only don't we have any luck,"
they sighed. "We have lost hope as well."

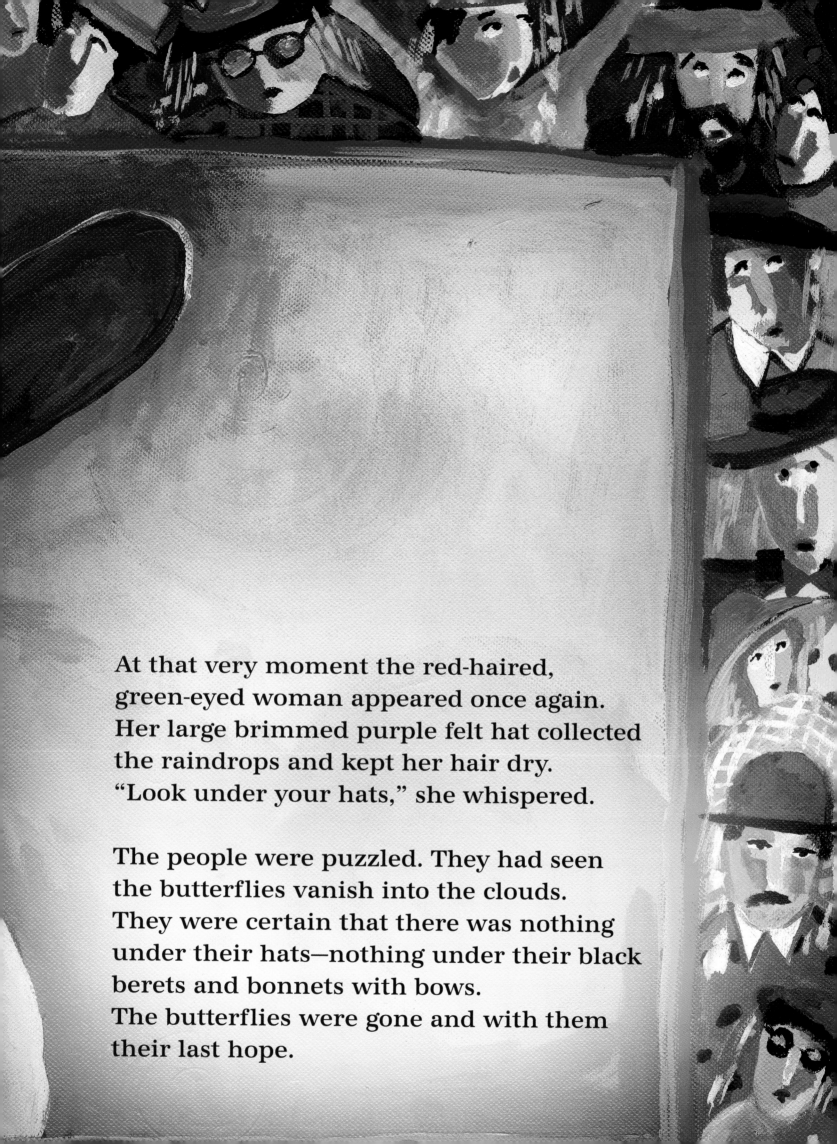

At that very moment the red-haired,
green-eyed woman appeared once again.
Her large brimmed purple felt hat collected
the raindrops and kept her hair dry.
"Look under your hats," she whispered.

The people were puzzled. They had seen
the butterflies vanish into the clouds.
They were certain that there was nothing
under their hats—nothing under their black
berets and bonnets with bows.
The butterflies were gone and with them
their last hope.

As quickly as the rains had come, they stopped.
The people lifted their hats—their fancy fur hats and
silly straw ones with feathers—and looked inside.
Just as they had thought, there were no butterflies.

"Look," they showed the mysterious woman,
"Nothing! There is nothing under our hats!"

"Look again," she whispered and then disappeared.

The people looked under their hats—
under their felt fedoras and high hats with polka dots.
They could hardly believe it.

The butterflies had gone, but they had left a trace . . . of something . . . a fine, faint powder. They saw it—the trace of the vanished butterflies. And that was all they needed—hope.

The people of Chelm
started building houses,
repairing sidewalks and
planting gardens.

Sometimes their roofs still
leaked and their sidewalks
still cracked, but not always.
Their gardens grew weeds
but also flowers.

The people of Chelm no longer looked for luck. They found something much better. And it was there, all along, right under their hats.